FIRST STORY

First Story's vision is a society that encourages and supports young people from all backgrounds to practise creative writing for pleasure, self-expression and agency. We believe everyone has a unique voice, a story to tell and a right to be heard. Our flagship programme places inspiring professional writers into secondary schools, where they work intensively with students and teachers to develop young people's creativity, confidence and ability. Through our core provision and extended opportunities, including competitions and events, participants develop skills to thrive in education and beyond.

Find out more at firststory.org.uk

First Story is a registered charity number 1122939 and a private company limited by guarantee incorporated in England with number 06487410. First Story is a business name of First Story Limited.

First published 2022 by First Story Limited
44 Webber Street, Southbank, London, SE1 8QW

www.firststory.org.uk

ISBN 978-0-85748-546-5

1 3 5 7 9 10 8 6 4 2

A CIP catalogue record for this book is available from the British Library.

Printed and bound in the UK by Aquatint
Typeset by Avon DataSet Ltd
Copy-edited by Alison Key
Proofread by Vivienne Heller
Cover designed by Simon Jones

The Rumours Were Right

An Anthology by the Year Eight First Story Group
at Beckfoot Oakbank School

<small>EDITED BY BEN MELLOR</small> | 2022

FIRST STORY

As Patron of First Story I am delighted that it continues to foster and inspire the creativity and talent of young people in secondary schools serving low-income communities.

I firmly believe that nurturing a passion for reading and writing is vital to the health of our country. I am therefore greatly encouraged to know that young people in this school – and across the country – have been meeting each week throughout the year in order to write together.

I send my warmest congratulations to everybody who is published in this anthology.

Camilla

HRH The Duchess of Cornwall

ACKNOWLEDGEMENTS

Melanie Curtis at Avon DataSet for her overwhelming support for First Story and for giving her time in typesetting this anthology.

Alison Key for copy-editing and Vivienne Heller for proofreading this anthology.

Simon Jones for designing the cover of this anthology.

Foysal Ali at Aquatint for printing this anthology at a discounted rate.

HRH The Duchess of Cornwall, Patron of First Story.

The Founders of First Story:
Katie Waldegrave and William Fiennes.

The Trustees of First Story:
Ed Baden-Powell (chair), Aziz Bawany, Aslan Byrne, Sophie Harrison, Sue Horner, Sarah Marshall, Bobby Nayyar, Jamie Waldegrave and Ella White.

First Story Ambassadors:
Patrice Lawrence MBE and Tracy Chevalier FRSL.

Thanks to our funders:
Jane & Peter Aitken, Amazon Literary Partnership, Authors' Licensing and Collecting Society (ALCS), Arts Council England, Tim Bevan & Amy Gadney, Fiona Byrd, The Blue Thread, Boots Charitable Trust, Fiona Byrd, Full House Literary Magazine, Garfield Weston Foundation, Goldsmith's Company Charity, John Lyons Charity, John R Murray Charitable Trust, Man Charitable Trust, Mercers' Company Charity, Paul Hamlyn Foundation, family and friends of Philip Pyke, ProWritingAid, RWHA Charity Fund, teamArchie, Wellington Management UK Foundation, Wordbank, the Friends of First Story and our regular supporters, individual donors and those who choose to remain anonymous.

Pro bono supporters and delivery partners including:
Arvon Foundation, BBC Teach, British Library, Cambridge University, Centre for Literacy in Primary Education, David Higham Associates, Driver Youth Trust, English and Media Centre, Forward Arts Foundation, Greenwich University, Hachette, Hull University, Huddersfield University, National Literacy Trust, Nottingham Trent University, Penguin Random House and Walker Books.

Most importantly we would like to thank the students, teachers and writers who have worked so hard to make First Story a success this year, as well as the many individuals and organisations (including those who we may have omitted to name) who have given their generous time, support and advice.

Contents

BIOGRAPHIES

ALICJA DOMAGALA: Food. Music. Phone.

AMELIA WARD-DANIEL: Animals. Netball. My friends.

AMY CHAMBERLAIN: Outside. Art. Animals.

BENJAMIN LAWRENCE: Books. Spaghetti. Gaming.

CHARLIE BROWN: Purple. Lasagne. Energetic.

CHARLIE WILKINSON: Keighley District Scouts Ron Powell Award
Winner 2022. Can rap at 11 syllables per second and ding at an E1.

DHUHA ALI: Love holidays, warm weather, family.

FAITH BAILEY: I like music. I like late-night walks. I like horror
movies and criminal movies.

FELICITY MELLER: Arches. Crystals. Chocolate.

GEORGE FELTON: McDonald's. White-chocolate Lindt balls. Home.

GRACE PRESCOTT: Art. Criminology. Photography.

IFRA KHAN: Shy. Lasagne. Blue.

IMOGEN UPTON: Tall. Yellow. Hat.

INAYA AHMED: Lashes. Dessert. Sarah.

JACK GRAHAM: Gaming. Clumsy. Funny.

JAYDEN BLACKLER: Football. Short. Nike.

KADEN O'NEILL: Liverpool FC, chocolate and dogs.

KAYDEN HORSFALL: Football. Family. Friends.

KEAVIE-LEIGH HALL: Netball. Dogs. Lucozade.

LEWIS PICKLES: If I could, I would definitely bring back the old Pringles mascot.

LOGAN SCARBOROUGH: Man United. Oakworth Cricket Club. Cars.

MYA WALSH: Football. Disney. Spanish.

PHOEBE CREWE: Christmas, Coco Pops, Covent Garden.

RONAN MARWOOD: Sofa. Lasagne. Gaming.

SARAH BEGUM: Inaya. Jewellery. Going on my phone.

SEBASTIAN WATTS: Player. Rugby. Confident.

SERAPHIM WESTON: Dramatic. Drama. Dogs.

SONNY JACKSON: Motorbikes. Family. Going out.

TOM HOLMES: Confidence. Karate. Xbox.

YUSUF AGDEMIR: Football. Clumsy. Leeds United.

Introduction

Ben Mellor, Writer-in-Residence

It's not always easy running writing workshops with a class of students as part of their school timetable: you hope that what you're offering will be more exciting than a regular English lesson, but you're keenly aware that the young people you're working with have not chosen to be working with you. You also know for certain that with any random selection of thirty children, there will be some, possibly many, in the class for whom writing is just not their bag.

Fortunately for me this Year Eight group were, for the most part, always up for whatever flights of fancy I asked them to go on with me – some of them even went on a few of their own completely unscheduled flights as well, which was a pleasure to see!

Thematically, we explored memories, connections to places and identity. But we also enjoyed letting our creativity run wild with open writing exercises involving the free association of random ideas.

I think this was most evident in the flash fiction workshops I ran. These involved the students attempting to tell a story in exactly one hundred words, in preparation for First Story's national 100-Word Story Competition. One of the students in this group, Alicja, is to be commended for having her story selected as one of the three from the whole school that was entered into that competition. But there were many writers in the class who put themselves forward and were good enough to be considered, and we really enjoyed the variety of styles and subject matter in evidence in the selection.

After such a difficult couple of years it was a pleasure to be able to offer this group of young people some time out of their regular English lessons to engage with the healing power of creativity. I believe that it is just as, if not more, important to their recovery and their education in general than any 'catch-up' curriculum.

The fun, enjoyment, thoughtfulness and imagination that was demonstrated over the course of our sessions together was testament to how vital creative practice is to learning and education. In just a short term's worth of working together I've noticed improvements in literacy, oracy, technical and creative writing skills and confidence.

I'm really proud of the work these young writers have created, and I hope they are too. I also hope that regardless of whether any of them decide to pursue careers in the arts in the future, all of them continue to be creative in whatever artistic media suit them best, purely for their own enjoyment and nourishment.

Teacher's Foreword

Ellie Brown, English Teacher and First Story Programme Lead

When I learned of the opportunity to have a writer come and work with my cohort of students, I was immediately excited. Knowing the students and their potential, as well as their imaginative personalities, I knew they would be able to create something special.

With each week came a new opening. The students thrived from the knowledge, expertise and enthusiasm that Ben brought to their sessions. Joy from every aspect, whether it be the team-building warm-up or the independent, focused crafting of work. It has been refreshing to witness students channel their opinions and voices into meaningful pieces. Their skills have been broadened, their minds opened and their passion ignited.

Alongside this, their sheer enjoyment has been excellent to see. They've faced fears in reading aloud to the class, undertaken leadership of peers, and supported and encouraged one another to achieve their personal best. Ultimately, they've left with skills and smiles, week in, week out.

This anthology highlights their character, talent and dedication to their creations. It's a pleasure to read and I hope you enjoy it as much as we have.

The Mission

Alicja Domagala

I walked through the oak doors. The cold night breeze swerving swiftly through my hair. My first mission. After three years studying and investigating in my spy school, I never thought I would be at this point. Gently placing my feet on the linoleum floors. I had to make this perfect. Suddenly I heard a deafening bang. Someone else was in the house. I should see what it was. Liz told me the house would be empty. Then I remembered that I was only here to get his diary. Nothing else. A few more steps. I glanced around me. Blood.

Where My Memories Come From

Alicja Domagala

My memories are the best thing in my life; there are some bad ones and many good ones. Most of those good ones come from my favourite place ever. This place is where I spend time with my family, where I have fun with my friends and sisters, where I grew up, where my personality came from and where I come from. In this place we have a massive garden. In my garden there's a barn. In the barn we have some cows and chickens. I collect eggs from there every morning at 6.45. The barn, on the side, has steps that lead to the loft where there are cubes of hay and straw – piles of it. Most of it is messed up around the space, because we had been jumping on it the other day. Outside the barn, there are a lot of garages. Inside these are my grandad's tractors and machines which he uses on the fields outside the house. In the summer we take out the two pools and my uncle blows them up for us. I love the smell of them when you first take them out of the box. We would make water slides from black foil running from the sides. They would always be hot if it was sunny. There are a lot more memories, sounds and smells in the best place but I wouldn't be able to explain it all. That's where my best memories come from.

The Key to My Chest

Alicja Domagala

Being me is like a book. When I'm closed, you see my blurb, the things I like, the things I do; you see me as the person you see every single day. But when you open the book, there are a lot of things I don't share. The pages are like a closed chest. The key to my chest is my best friend. No one else could have the power to open it. I know it will never be opened, but it contains embarrassment, sadness, happiness and something like pride. My feelings and emotions are like the ocean hiding everything that's at the bottom of it; the waves blocking everyone out except my best friend. The key to my chest.

The Haunted

Amelia Ward-Daniel

I sat there staring at the TV. Emotionless. Waiting for the news flash. But then I saw police going past. I got up. Was it him? I opened my door – I saw a lifeless figure get carried out of house 27. Their face still had pure horror strained on it. I went back inside; I didn't dare watch. The news came on. The Scarer is back. I couldn't think. Fear washed over me. Scratch. Scratch. I ran to the basement. Then I thought, had I locked the door? It swung open. I tried to get up. I was too late.

Nightmare

Amelia Ward-Daniel

I walked down the alleyway. Blood stained my hands. What had I done? I bolted to my house and slammed the door shut. I stood leaning on the wall. My eyes darted in every direction. I spun around looking desperately for the sink. I began rinsing my hands but the blood wouldn't come off. Come on. Come on. Come on. I let out a scream.

But I woke up.

I acted like the 'dream' hadn't happened. But deep down I knew it had. It's all I could think about. I wanted to get out of my own head. Memories flashed in my mind, black and white, and then they were gone. I told myself it was a nightmare. I headed back to the place where I thought it had happened in my nightmare. Then I saw it. It all came back. What had happened last night. Everything. Flashing before my eyes at full speed. I wanted it to stop. 'Stop!' I screamed… I had killed someone. With… With my mind? What?? Voices whispered in my head, 'You're evil. Evil!' How could I have done this? I can't kill people with my mind, it's impossible.

But I had.

Evil…

Evil…

Evil…

It was replaying in my mind repeatedly. Over and over again.

Overpowering my head. I couldn't take it. I could kill things with my mind.

Murderer…

Murderer…

Murderer…

Darkness. I was dead.

Anti-Social

Amy Chamberlain

People crowded every inch of the floor in the school grounds, which made me petrified. It was my first day of school. My anxiety was through the roof and my heartbeat got quicker, quicker and quicker. I saw a patch of space on the other side of the pitch, I was determined to get there. Halfway through my voyage I panicked as I was shoved roughly. I looked up as my eyes met a hand reaching out to me. I took the person's hand and they led me out of the terrible crowd. That's how I met my best friend.

The Destruction of a Forest

Benjamin Lawrence

I listened to the gentle rustling of the leaves on the great oak
    trees, wondering how old they are.
I listened to the whirring and buzzing of chainsaws and then
    the booming sound of falling trees.
I listened to the tweeting and chirping of the dying species of
    birds defending their nests.
I listened to the cracking and popping of the fire burning each
    tree in a raging inferno of hatred.
I listened to the men shouting and cutting.
I listened to the destruction of an enormous forest.

The Dinosaur

Benjamin Lawrence

There was a dinosaur. He ate his bread on the highway with a fork. He enjoyed it very much but, alas, it was poisoned. So, the dinosaur set off on an adventure to collect the antidote! He never found the antidote and eventually succumbed to the poison... Then a wizard found him and revived him and also showed him the way to where the antidote was. He said that a rare giant bird had it.

The Land of the Upside-Down

Charlie Brown

It was the summer of 2022 and it was time for a holiday. Australia. I was a bit unsure at first from people saying it's an upside-down country but it just added to the sun. We arrived after a long flight but I won't bore you with the trip. As it turns out, the rumours were right. I got off the plane and as I entered the airport everything was the wrong way round. It was like I had inverted controls, like I was controlling myself through mirrored vision. Still now I remember everything, having flashbacks and memories, everyone else was walking like it was normal. So I tried. Deep down I know that either everyone thought it was strange and was trying to fit in or it was normal. I'll never be the same.

Don't mind that.

The End

Charlie Wilkinson

BANG!! The gunshot was fired with a deafening sound. I came crashing to the ground with a loud thud. Slowly I closed my eyes and began to reflect. I watched on as my life flashed before me. All the good times, all the bad times, and all the downright awful times. I watched on as light turned to dark, and tried to deny what was happening. As time got slower and slower, I realised I had nowhere else to go so I finally accepted it. This was the end of me.

Attachment

Dhuha Ali

Lucy's best friend was her dog, Bella. The pair were attached to each other, they always went on walks together (it was their favourite thing to do). Lucy even sat Bella with her for eating. But Lucy's parents recently said they wanted to move to Spain, which was fine, but Bella wasn't coming. Lucy's heart was torn to bits. She decided to take Bella out on their last walk before Bella had to say goodbye to Lucy and stay with her Aunty Shelby. While they were walking, Lucy let go of Bella's leash and disappeared. Bella returned to Lucy's parents without Lucy and she was never seen again.

Faith

Faith Bailey

My name is Faith.
My name comes from my mother.
In Greek, my name means: confidence, trust, belief.
I have many nicknames.
My name would be white or silver.
My name would taste like cookie-dough ice-cream.
If my name were a number, it would be five.

The Blue Moon

Felicity Meller

I ran home, straight into the woods with the wolf hot on my heels. I ran to my log cabin and he tackled me. 'Luke!' I laughed as the so-called 'menacing wolf' flopped on top of me in a heap. I got up and grabbed a blanket. I set off to a hill with Luke at my side. I lay down at the top and looked up at the stars.

The Morning

George Felton

As the boy walks down his eerie stairs, he feels a small cold breeze. He gets to the bottom of the cracked, over-used chairs and then realises… where are his parents? Suddenly he panics. His parents weren't upstairs in bed and he has checked the whole house. What's happened to them? The one thing that comes straight to his thirteen-year-old's brain is, 'Did they leave me?' It is 9 a.m. My parents never get up till 10 a.m.,' he whispers. Then he starts shouting, 'MUM! DAD! WHERE ARE YOU?' It doesn't work. No one answers.

Empty Box

George Felton

I feel like an empty box,
My skin feels like chickenpox.
I'm dead inside
When I get forced to play outside.
I am depressed,
And very stressed.
But when it comes to skiing,
I feel I can die being
The best person I am.
But my heart is bigger than a dam.

Chaos in Town

Grace Prescott

Keighley is where I was born, with schools and parks.
It's where I feel almost trapped, as I feel that if I am to be free
    I will be alone.
This is the place where anything can happen, good or bad.
People running riots or shopping like they're all friends.
The place where the black velvet skies and diamante stars
    don't come around.
We are showered with rain, snow, and hail that feels like stones
Pelting down.

Smile for the Camera

Grace Prescott

Two siblings, one boy and one girl, were as adventurous as anything. They decided one day they were going to go on a walk in the woods. They knew their curfew. They arrived in the woods by 9 p.m. and wandered around for a bit. Upon entering the woods they had noticed pictures of people on trees and on the ground. But not ordinary people – these people had jet-black eyes and faces as blank as paper. They heard strange noises as they went deeper. The next thing they knew, a guy was staring at them and the last words they heard were: 'smile for the camera.'

Home Is...

Ifra Khan

Home is a place that is soft and warm
Home is a place where I can express myself
Home is a place to feel safe
Home is a delightful place
Home is a calm place
A home is a place built with love, kindness and bricks

Feelings

Ifra Khan

At first you start as an empty box in a small dark corner
You want
To destroy everything
To annoy everybody
To sink

Then you start
To live
To laugh
To love
To be happy
To float
To explore

And then
To relax.

My Sisters

Imogen Upton

My sisters,
one dark hair,
one brown curls,
walking side by side,
mountains in the distance,
a comfy sofa in front of the TV,
a glowing garden,
my sisters.

My sisters,
gold eyes in the sun,
tangles of hair,
swish, swish, swish,
doing makeovers with crap makeup,
cinnamon rolls,
ginger cookies,
my sisters.

A Certain Way

Imogen Upton

There was a certain way she walked,
Sort of strutting but a bit calmer.
It made the road light up behind her.
Bioluminescent footsteps.

There was a certain way he talked,
Sort of growly and very deep.
It made his words trail behind him.
Fiery taunts and curses.

There was a certain way she sang,
Sort of like a morning lark.
She made music dance around her.
Glowing notes.

There was a certain way he played,
Sort of beautiful and graceful.
He made piano keys play along with him.
A chorus of keys.

There is a certain way I write,
Sort of terrible but funny.
I leave scribbles in my wake.
Red crosses on the page.

Shards of Me

Imogen Upton

To break a glass sculpture and reveal a glow within,
To watch the cracks widen and show the real you,
Not the scrunched-up note or the sodden cardboard
on the outside,
To answer the question,
Who am I meant to be?
To share the secret in corners of rooms,
To destroy the actor you've come to know yourself as,
To feel the cool marble underneath the glass,
To cry out at the insanity of the crystal on the floor,
To swim in the fountain of your tears,
To step over the overflowing bin of memories,
And to watch the rotting tree sprout new glass leaves,
To patch up the broken window you once were,
To crush the gloss of your outer shell into sand,
To laugh at the sound of the crunch,
To look down at the fragile self you once were,
To rub out the pencil scribbles of life.

Smile for the Camera – I

Inaya Ahmed

As I walked down the road, cautiously, a loud bang smacked through my ears. What was it? My heart was pounding but yet I had the nerve to look behind. There was nothing there!

As time passed by, I got home to lightning striking on my window (bang!). It was blinding me! Carefully, I shut my curtains with no bother at all. I walked to the kitchen for my mouth-watering dinner when I heard a strange knock from my creaky door.

As terrified as I was, I peeked through the gap of my door but no one was there. I spun round to a tall man covered in black clothing. I questioned his coming and I heard nothing but pure silence. My hands were shaking. My lips were trembling.

Smile for the Camera – II

Inaya Ahmed

I had to make this perfect
A patch of space
Avoided social contact
When I was nervous to start
'Smile for the camera'
Eyes go gold in the sun
Sunrise in the morning
Still not got
Hours became days, days became weeks, weeks became months
On no account can people copy this.

The Nightshift

Jack Graham

Late one winter there was a night guard working late and suddenly he got a call from his boss. He was asking if he was okay and if he was safe. He said he was fine and hung up. A few minutes later he heard a huge bang and was horrified when he checked the cameras to see animatronics sprinting towards his office. He slammed the doors shut and was safe... for now. Was all this a nightmare? His job was safe, right? Then he remembered the air vent. Oh no...

Surprise

Jayden Blackler

As the wind howls down and lightning lights the sky, I enter an abandoned house. Darkness covers the rooms as I look around. Creaks and footsteps can be heard upstairs. As I walk upstairs the footsteps get louder and louder, and blood drops are all over the floor leading to one room. There is an eerie feeling in the air, something suspicious. Suddenly a group of ten people jump out and scream, 'SURPRISE! HAPPY BIRTHDAY!' It was all a surprise birthday party.

The Explosion on the Plane – Chapter 1

Kaden O'Neill

Boarding the plane, I knew something was not right; the plane was suspicious. I knew something was wrong. We were heading for Santorini, in Greece. The plane took off, but it was very shaky. There was a faint beeping noise – it seemed to be coming from the distance. Possibly from the toilets. Shortly afterwards, a fire was followed by a bang. The plane started to rapidly lose altitude.

The Boy

Kayden Horsfall

The boy ran into the woods in the dawn of night after a white figure that was running at a pace. He was halfway in and got worried. The birds tweeting, sticks snapping under his feet. He saw it again. The boy sprinted towards it. It disappeared. He heard the big clock strike midnight and realised he was lost. Hours became days, days became weeks, weeks became months. Feasting and drinking whatever he could. The howl from a pack of wolves echoed through the woods. The boy never returned home.

Attached

Keavie-Leigh Hall

There was a young boy, his name was Archie. He didn't talk much and often avoided social contact. The only thing he talked to was a small animal, not the usual house pet, it was indeed a hedgehog.

Life's a Funny Place

Lewis Pickles

Life's a funny place,
I remember a dream,
A patch of space,
The rumours were right,
Hours became days, days became weeks,
Sunrise in the morning,
Cutting half my hair off,
When I was nervous to start,
When I would fall over everything,
The marks and scratches told me everything,
When I couldn't care less,
When life wasn't a mess...

My Name Is

Logan Scarborough

My name is Logan.
My name comes from my mum's favourite movie.
My cousins call me LJ.
My name sounds like Logen.
My name is red.
My name would be a shark.
My name would taste like grapes.
My name is Logan.

Day

Mya Walsh

The day had finally come. The day we had all been dreading for months. Driving in the car, suitcases all piled up. It began to get real. As we approached the airport terminal my eyes welled up. Ambling up to the sliding doors, people walking out with all different things going on. After all the bags were checked in, it was finally time. Time for them to go. My eyes filled up even more and burst like an over-used water pipe. They walked away. I couldn't breathe. That was it. Not to be seen again for four years. The tears kept flowing for hours. Goodbye.

My Name Is

Phoebe Crewe

My name is Phoebe.
My name comes from my mum.
In Greek, my name means the shining one.
I have many nicknames.
My name is bright pink or silver.
My name would taste like chocolate ice-cream.
If my name were a number, it would be zero.

My Name Is

Ronan Marwood

My name is Ronan.
A rotten and fluffy dung beetle
on a skyscraper wearing rip-off
Nikes called Hikeys with a fish
instead of a tick.
My name is Ronan.

The Librarian

Sarah Begum

One day, the young boy got into trouble with a teacher because he'd been running around the corridors with his friends having a water fight in school. He was told to go to the library after school detention. He entered the library and a book flew past his face. 'Hello?' the boy said. He saw no one there and decided to leave. The doors locked. He tried to leave when suddenly something tapped him on his shoulder. It was the librarian. She chanted a spell that trapped him in a book called *The Young Boy Who Had Disappeared*. He was stuck there for ever. The librarian told people that he had got hit by a bus on the way home and was killed.

The Crack in the Wall

Sebastian Watts

There was a boy with a massive crack in his walls. He could see his neighbours. The boy was able to put a PlayStation in there but the crack was from an earthquake so he was afraid to try. One day another earthquake happened. He could surely see his neighbours now, but he forgot he had none. But he was able to see the cars driving past, at least. So one day he decided to get it fixed. It had started to annoy him, because when it snowed or rained it all leaked in. So he got it fixed.

Memories

Seraphim Weston

Before my grandfather died
I remember he used to sit in his ruffled beige
throne. He'd sit for hours. Hours of just watching the fire.
Misty, their family beagle, would lie on the silk carpet looking
 up at him.
When I was four, I used to play with building blocks, piling
 them up to make the tallest tower. He'd sit there waiting for
 it to tumble and when it did, he'd help me build another.
After four years I don't know what or how to feel.

You

Seraphim Weston

Not everyone finds life easy.
Many people feel isolated.
Like a small drifted boat in the big sea.
A single letter on a blank page.
A chicken in a flock of swans.
For others that's not the case.
But you. You aren't like the others.
You are special.
You are unique.

Butterflies

Seraphim Weston

They're just there. Free.
Floating in the atmosphere.
My favourite species,
The genus *morpho*.
When it rains their wings
Glisten and glow.
Bright blue.

My grandfather was obsessed
With studying them.
Sat in the garden watching them.
Next to the field.
I'd watch them too.
It made me feel free too.

How Quickly Things Can Change

Sonny Jackson

On a cold Tuesday morning, December 25th 2013 at 8.34 a.m., a young boy dramatically runs down the stairs at the speed of light to open presents. Ten presents gone and he has still not got what he wanted. Fifteen presents gone and he has still not got what he wanted. One more is left. Will he get it? Will he be heartbroken? He opens it as his heart rate rises and he screams out of happiness. He has got roller-skates after two years of waiting. He begs his mum, 'Can I go to the lake?' And only because it's Christmas she says he can. As they arrive, he sprints towards the lake, dying to skate around. He sings, he jumps, he's never been happier until CRACK! SPLASH! The ice breaks. He falls. The stream takes him away. His parents turn around, only to realise he's not there and they think it's all their fault.

Running*

Tom Holmes

Darkness. Cold. Package. The wind blows vigorously in his face. The Nike backpack filled with one item. Dark alleys. Paranoid. He runs with the wind into the clear open sky and then down a tight alley. Men. Bats. Precautious, he slips the package under a rock with a note. A clip of money − £500. Sprinting. Police. Sirens wailing, getting nearer, nearer, nearer, and then. Tyres screeching. Police shouting. He tries to run but gets nowhere, the police try to grab him. He picks up a bat. Thud. Unconscious. Running.

*All places, names, activities are fictional and not based on real events. Copyright claims will be fined £20. On no exception can people copy this unless it is in the anthology for First Story. Ts & Cs apply.

What's the Point?

Tom Holmes

Why stay here,
What is the point?
Stop being as cracked as a shell
Or smashed like a mirror,
Go and break your fixed mould,
Go spin like a wheel,
Launch like a ball,
Find a new beginning
Through an open door,
Don't be so boring,
Why fix your joints?
What's the point?

Strange Dream

Yusuf Agdemir

I sat down, menacingly staring at the wall. It was like it was telling me a story. The marks and scratches told me everything about the past and what it had been through. It held wisdom of the past, like it was ancient. It brought me into a whole new world, making me want to explore its life. It was like reading a horror book, it had been through so much, seen life and death. I almost passed out. Then, I woke up.

Untitled Feelings

Yusuf Agdemir

Emotions can be like brick walls and bricks,
Hidden from the world and no one can see.
They can also be like glass windows and taps –
You can see the emotions and what the person is going
    through in their life.

We Remember

Group Poem

I remember the first time I walked – my dad bribed me with a
piece of watermelon.

I remember the long nights before my birthday in the
morning.

I remember smelling the bakery outside the Co-op every day.

I remember when I got pushed into a wall, my teeth went
black.

I remember when me and my dad went to Cliffe Castle and
we both ate Screwball ice-creams.

I remember when I got lost in Asda.

I remember the bright yellow stairs at Peppa Pig World. I had
a paddy on them.

I remember when I got my face painted to look like a butterfly.

I remember baking my first cake all by myself during
lockdown.

I remember playing on the 2p slot machines in Blackpool.

I remember jumping up and down in the waves at Bondi.

I remember when I first smelled the salty sea water.

I remember watching my sister's eyes go gold in the sun.

I remember when my brother had a shard of glass in his foot.

I remember when my baby cousin pooed on me the first time I
held him.

He was thankfully clothed.

I remember accidentally calling my teacher 'Mum' in primary.

I remember when I trapped my thumb atrociously in the car
door.

I remember getting fifty out of fifty on a Year Four maths test.

I remember the leaving day Year Six, when everyone had their leavers' hoodies and were signing each other's books.

I remember the first time I cried about football.

I remember punching my friend in the face.

I remember when a spider was in my bed and tickled my feet.
I was scared.

I remember a dream I had which was about lions – they killed
me and I woke up.

I remember not being able to move one morning as I watched
a black shadow move gracefully towards me.

I remember before my grandfather died he used to sit in his
ruffled beige throne.

I remember the sunrise in the morning.

FIRST STORY

First Story's vision is a society that encourages and supports young people from all backgrounds to practise creative writing for pleasure, self-expression and agency. We believe everyone has a unique voice, a story to tell and a right to be heard. Our flagship programme places inspiring professional writers into secondary schools, where they work intensively with students and teachers to develop young people's creativity, confidence and ability. Through our core provision and extended opportunities, including competitions and events, participants develop skills to thrive in education and beyond.

Find out more at firststory.org.uk

First Story is a registered charity number 1122939 and a private company limited by guarantee incorporated in England with number 06487410. First Story is a business name of First Story Limited.

First published 2022 by First Story Limited
44 Webber Street, Southbank, London, SE1 8QW

www.firststory.org.uk

ISBN 978-0-85748-546-5

1 3 5 7 9 10 8 6 4 2

A CIP catalogue record for this book is available from the British Library.

Printed and bound in the UK by Aquatint
Typeset by Avon DataSet Ltd
Copy-edited by Alison Key
Proofread by Vivienne Heller
Cover designed by Simon Jones

Killed by the Coconut, not by the Shark

An Anthology by the Epic Extras First Story Group
at Beckfoot Oakbank School

Edited by Ben Mellor | 2022

FIRST STORY

As Patron of First Story I am delighted that it continues to foster and inspire the creativity and talent of young people in secondary schools serving low-income communities.

I firmly believe that nurturing a passion for reading and writing is vital to the health of our country. I am therefore greatly encouraged to know that young people in this school – and across the country – have been meeting each week throughout the year in order to write together.

I send my warmest congratulations to everybody who is published in this anthology.

Camilla

HRH The Duchess of Cornwall

ACKNOWLEDGEMENTS

Melanie Curtis at Avon DataSet for her overwhelming support for First Story and for giving her time in typesetting this anthology.

Alison Key for copy-editing and Vivienne Heller for proofreading this anthology.

Simon Jones for designing the cover of this anthology.

Foysal Ali at Aquatint for printing this anthology at a discounted rate.

HRH The Duchess of Cornwall, Patron of First Story.

The Founders of First Story:
Katie Waldegrave and William Fiennes.

The Trustees of First Story:
Ed Baden-Powell (chair), Aziz Bawany, Aslan Byrne, Sophie Harrison, Sue Horner, Sarah Marshall, Bobby Nayyar, Jamie Waldegrave and Ella White.

First Story Ambassadors:
Patrice Lawrence MBE and Tracy Chevalier FRSL.

Thanks to our funders:
Jane & Peter Aitken, Amazon Literary Partnership, Authors' Licensing and Collecting Society (ALCS), Arts Council England, Tim Bevan & Amy Gadney, Fiona Byrd, The Blue Thread, Boots Charitable Trust, Fiona Byrd, Full House Literary Magazine, Garfield Weston Foundation, Goldsmith's Company Charity, John Lyons Charity, John R Murray Charitable Trust, Man Charitable Trust, Mercers' Company Charity, Paul Hamlyn Foundation, family and friends of Philip Pyke, ProWritingAid, RWHA Charity Fund, teamArchie, Wellington Management UK Foundation, Wordbank, the Friends of First Story and our regular supporters, individual donors and those who choose to remain anonymous.

Pro bono supporters and delivery partners including:
Arvon Foundation, BBC Teach, British Library, Cambridge
University, Centre for Literacy in Primary Education, David Higham
Associates, Driver Youth Trust, English and Media Centre, Forward
Arts Foundation, Greenwich University, Hachette, Hull University,
Huddersfield University, National Literacy Trust, Nottingham Trent
University, Penguin Random House and Walker Books.

Most importantly we would like to thank the students, teachers and
writers who have worked so hard to make First Story a success this
year, as well as the many individuals and organisations (including
those who we may have omitted to name) who have given their
generous time, support and advice.

Contents

BIOGRAPHIES

ALIMA BEGUM: Confident. Sincere. Shy.

ANIQA BEGUM: Imaginative. Outspoken/bold/audacious. Witty.

ANISAH ALI (BKG): Bubbly. Sweet. The better Anisah.

ANISAH ALI (VCH): Amazing. Kind. Material girl.

CALEB CROSSLEY HARVEY: Kind, confident and thoughtful.

CHARLOTTE VARGA: Independent. Kind. Helpful.

CHLOE GREEN: Kind, geeky, passionate.

DECLAN MULDERRIG: Nerdy. Helpful. Quiet.

ENYAW McCOMB: Imaginative. Sarcastic. Geeky.

ESME GARBUTT: Confident. Optimistic. Happy :)

EVIE KNEESHAW: Unique. Quirky. Pretty cool.

EVIE PATTISON: Average. Smart. No sense of smell.

EVIE SHUTTLEWORTH: Roller skating. Goblins. Lemurs.

FAIZA ALI: Hijabi. Gorgeous. Modest.

FINLAY STOKER: Napping. Iced coffee. Experiences.

IMAAN UL HAQ: Maths. Art. Olivia Rodrigo.

ISAA UL HAQ: Stoma. Kind. Amazing!

ISABELLA CURTIS: Books. Musicals. Taylor Swift.

KAYDI-LOU WALTON: Quack, splash, chirp.

NADIA KHANUM: Short, very cute, Bengali.

NEVE GARBUTT: Nerdy, loud, funny – I like to think so.

POPPY HOWARD: Hard-working, ambitious, quiet.

RIFHA HAQUE: Imaginative, creative, arty.

TJ ATKINSON: Funny. Weird. Cheesy.

Introduction

Ben Mellor, Writer-in-Residence

When I first delivered a year-long residency at Beckfoot Oakbank in 2019 our after-school group had, on average, around eight to ten young people showing up each week. During this term-long residency (my first time back at the school since the pandemic), I was amazed at a turn-out of around thirty young people for our first after-school session. I was even more amazed the following week when nearly all of them came back, some even bringing friends!

Whilst I'd like to flatter myself that this was because of what a brilliant workshop leader I am, I believe that it's more a case of how hungry young people are for a creative outlet, now more than ever.

To have the space to explore your thoughts about yourself and your relationship with other people and the world, and to shape those thoughts into creative expressions that will be professionally published and archived, is an incredibly valuable opportunity for anyone, but particularly those who find themselves at the formative age that these young people are. It's an opportunity I wish I'd had more of when I was their age, and one that I'm so pleased to be able to offer through working with First Story.

Many of the young people in this anthology were discovering writing for the first time in our sessions, while some were bringing creative practices they'd already begun to hone elsewhere. In fact, some had even been published in other anthologies when they were younger! But regardless of what experience they were entering the room with, all of the writers published here engaged in the games and exercises that made up our sessions with enthusiasm, humour, vulnerability, openness and imagination.

I was constantly impressed by the perceptiveness, honesty and originality with which they considered and discussed the pieces of writing I brought in to use as a stimulus. And I was equally impressed by the vibrancy, uniqueness and variety of their creative responses.

I was particularly proud of the fact that two of the writers in this group, Finlay and Esme, wrote pieces of flash fiction that were not only selected for entry in First Story's national 100-Word Story Competition but won places − Esme's was a runner up and Finlay's won second place!

But regardless of success or otherwise in competitions, I'm most proud of this group for simply choosing to give up their own time after school to show up week in, week out and be part of a community of fellow creatives. Whether or not any of them choose to pursue careers in the creative industries, and I've no doubt that many of them could, my main hope is that these young writers continue to write, and read, and make whatever other types of art bring them pleasure.

Being creative, particularly telling stories, is a fundamental part of being human. It's a fact that is often forgotten as we get older, sometimes sadly as a result of the education system, reinforced by work, government and society. I sincerely hope that these young writers hold on to and nurture their creative sparks throughout their lives. When you read the quality of their work, I'm sure you'll agree that they should, not just for their own benefit, but for the world's.

Teacher's Foreword

Ellie Brown, English Teacher and First Story Programme Leader

When the opportunity to lead this great programme arose, I jumped at the chance to be involved. I love creative writing that has meaning and purpose, and the chance to engage some of our brilliant students in my passion has been wonderful.

The great thing about young people is that they all have such an individual, independent voice yet sometimes this remains untapped – the chance to hear their voice is sometimes missed. The platform provided by Ben and First Story has enabled these students to realise their voice is important to enrich the community they choose to share it with. They write with confident, authentic voices and have uncompromising flair that reflects their individuality.

Through the programme, students have bonded over warm-ups, listened to each other's stories and experiences, and shared hopes and fears. They have been able to connect with themselves and each other in a relaxed, safe environment – a joy after months spent apart at home.

It was incredible to see masses of students gathering at the first session when they opted to take part in the programme: different year groups but united in their passion for writing. Throughout, we have been lucky enough to hear about a multitude of important topics, themes and ideas, all chosen and shaped with care and experience. Each writer has something unique and promising about their work; I believe this to be just the beginning for some of our young people on their writing journey.

This anthology of work is a reflection of the effort, commitment, and talent of our young people. It has been a pleasure to be a part of and I hope you enjoy it as much as we have.

Red Flower

Alima Begum

The meadow, far past the road and city. It was designated in the far end of the forest behind some terraced houses. It was peaceful, a great place to run and let your mind out. Did you notice the 'was'? A red liquid dripped on the flowers immediately. The first thought that came was 'blood'. You meaninglessly wandered further. You kept your guard high. That was until a horrific smell hit you. It smelled like something rotten. You halted. Did you really want to go further? Further past the oak tree with a dying smell to it?

The Phoenix

Aniqa Begum

The sirens went off.

The crowd was sent into an immediate panic and I grabbed the cross, as the attention on me was gone.

I slipped past security who had their guns trained on the crowd, ready for anything. I escaped the room with ease and my hand tucked loose strands of hair behind my ear. The cross was tucked in my purse and just as I was going to leave, a gun cocked behind me.

I turned around and I was met with dark brown eyes. I was taken aback by his overall appearance, his messy yet tamed, dark hair, the tattoos trailing up his neck. My eyes widened as I recognised him.

'How are you still alive?' His question made my heart flutter, his voice was so low and hypnotic. I didn't answer him and then some knocks on the door startled the both of us.

Enjoyment

Anisah Ali (BKG)

I love to sleep in my bed,
To write the things in my head,
To colour something easy,
To annoy my sister
and wait for her to tell my mum I hit her,
To talk to my friend
and then end up in a call that never ends,
To read an interesting book
and end up staring into the crannies and nooks.
All these things I enjoy and do
for my pleasure.

Who I Am

Anisah Ali (VCH)

My name is Anisah
I love doing art
My nickname is Allu Bay
I love eating food and staying at home
I hate the smell of tuna
I love the phrase 'material girl'
I went on holiday when I was seven
Stayed in Bangladesh for one month
Came back looking like a tomato
And went to bed.

My Friends

Caleb Crossley Harvey

My friends are my light.
When the light is dim
they are there to fix the light,
to make it bright again,
to make me feel happy
when it's severely damaged,
when it's lost the brightness
and won't shine again.

My Home

Caleb Crossley Harvey

Home is the fish and chips from the fisheries,
the best ones are at the beach.
I remember when I was little,
the smell of fresh fish and chips
being served to kids, half price.
I liked the sound of that
so I quickly went and got some.
The taste was great,
but I do not know
what happened after –
I hope it was fun.

Rosie Comes to Stay

Charlotte Varga

We'd taken her in, tried to sort her out, stop her from being nosy. She didn't listen...

The walls of the tunnel rushed past us as we raced down it, the trees whispering their secrets. Flying out on to the cushions we saw our friends who lived in the trees and the ladder that would lead to our demise.

This wasn't supposed to happen, I was supposed to keep her safe. She found a loophole in our gazes. She'd run off, tried to stick her nose where it didn't belong. We can't go back now. It's impossible to escape from here...

Demon

Charlotte Varga

Walking along the grimy pavement, turning the corner. Feeling my bare feet hit the stone and glass. My right foot was swollen now, making it hard to walk. The shard of the authentic crystal hippo still stuck out. It didn't hurt. Nothing ever hurt me. 'Demon', they called me. Shouting nasty remarks. It only happened because I had put my hand under the wheel of a bus. I wanted to feel pain. It didn't work. It never worked. They kicked me out. I don't know why. Did they also think I was a demon? Was I ruining their reputation?

Home

Charlotte Varga

Home.
A strange word.
Often associated with where we live.
But it's more than that...
The warm blanket that you curl up under in winter,
the small furry lump of cat that crawls on you and annoys you
    to no end,
but is comforting at the same time,
and the smell of freshly baked cakes filling up the air,
as the soft tune of a piano flows through the background.
This is home.

My Name Is...

Chloe Green

My name is Chloe.
It's pink and green
and sort of suits me.
It's French and Greek,
From old mythologies,
The name of the goddess
of family and grass.
I have a few other names:
Lolo, Coco.
In Spain they might call me Loco but
My name is Chloe.

Home Is

Declan Mulderrig

Home is a place of solitude and being comfy,
Home is the place for you and your family,
Home is the place where you play with brothers,
Home is the place where you're looked after by your mother.

Home is the place where you can do what you want to do,
Home is different from the place where you learn two plus two,
Home is the place where the heart is,
Home is the place where you don't have to worry
about annoying things or annoying kids.

Home is a place where you are protected,
Home is where you cannot be detected,
Home is the place where the bad things go away,
Home is the place where you and your friends play.

Home is the place where you and your siblings fight,
Home is the place where you are protected in the night,
Home is where you can have fun,
Home is the place where you can sit outside and enjoy the sun.

Home is the origin of your childhood memories,
Home is where you reminisce about what could have been,
Home is the place where you argued with your dad and mum,
Home is… no, was, the place you had to move on from.

What Object Represents You?

Declan Mulderrig

People always ask, what kind of person are you?
Usually you respond with words, emotions, but there is
    something
that is better than those two.
Objects can be so representative, sometimes better than
    words –
for example, you can be an egg – very fragile – or a ball –
    very sporty.

You may say that you are trapped inside a cage,
or you may feel like your paintbrush is limited.
You may say that video games are your life.
Maybe you need a bed that follows you all day.

Sometimes you don't know how to express yourself.
You may say that the long corridor of life is unfair,
or that in life there are too many worksheets,
but you've only just started looking at the world from your
    bird's nest.

For me, it's easy, I know what I am,
but for you, well… You need to work that out yourself.
So, what object represents you?

I Am

Declan Mulderrig

I am an egg – very fragile and shy.
I am a picture – very perfect (or at least I try).
I am a lion – fierce and strong.
I am a wise man – often not wrong.

I am free and hopeful – I am a dove.
I am a broken heart – can never find love.
I am a controller – I am attached to it.
I am a dumbbell – very fit.

I am a Pokémon nerd – I am proud of it.
I am a paintbrush – very creative.
I am a pen and paper – I work extremely hard.
I am a trash bag – not wanted. Now I am scarred.

I am the object no one can remember.
I am the snow – playful in December.
I am a skeleton costume – very scary and spooky.
I am a table – I have no friends. I am lonely.

What It Is

Enyaw McComb

To listen to those who have tape over their mouths,
who refuse to peel the tape away with their fingernails,
To help those out of the box
that they have unfortunately confined themselves to,
To cry sometimes to show those who believe it's weak
that crying is the strongest thing one can do,
To see those who need help and tell them
that it gets better eventually,
To daydream about running through flower fields,
To play around with words and create a world of my own,
To smile and to laugh,
To care,
That's what it is to be me.
How about you?

Apprehension

Enyaw McComb

A steel spike scraping against the wall. His cavalier attitude making a display against the already tattered brick of the wall. A high-pitched sound escaped from his lips and hid in the crevice of the kingdom we call ears. Or was that the ringing making its second debut? The scraping had hindered, but the rustling had quickened, his relentless pace. Closeness becoming apparent by the small tugs of pain on the fabric, compromising my movement.

Gross Expectations

Esme Garbutt

At the fitting, they prodded me with needles. Sharp pricks left specks of blood on the inner lining. It surprised me to see blood, that I was still alive. I'd felt dead since we got engaged. I could only imagine what married life would be like. Layers of white silk poured down my legs, lace tangled in my hair, a sharp dip crossed my cleavage. The bodice, plastered with pearls and glistening ribbons, crushed my lungs. Ribbons wrapped around my neck. I felt trapped; the cooking, the cleaning. My hands reached for my soon-to-be swollen belly, the child growing inside.

Love

Esme Garbutt

I really like loving someone, but only loving them.
I don't like feeling responsible for their guilt,
for their anger, for their sadness.
I don't like the worry that it could all be taken
from me, so I destroy it before it has the chance
to leave. I don't like the dread of seeing them unhappy,
I don't like the thought I'm doing something wrong.
I like being in love, but it's almost always better when
the person you love doesn't know.

S-t-i-t-c-h

Evie Kneeshaw

She had the hourglass figure of a goddess. Wide hips that swayed as she walked and round breasts that bounced at every step. Eyes an enchanting hazel that stared through your soul. Long, black, oily hair that cascaded down her back. And lips as red as blood. Her name is Griffin.

She sat there innocently, stirring a glass of red wine with her finger.

'I'm sorry, Rain.'

Her gaze fixed on the lifeless body in front of her. She wiped her blood-stained lips.

'I really liked you.'

Griffin placed her glass down and stepped out of the window.

House of Mirrors

Evie Pattison

Our house was old, too old. I hated it. It was haunted. I know it was haunted because one night it was too cold, so I got up to get more blankets for my bed. That's when I saw her. Holding a book, she looked like me. But like my shadow. She saw me, then disappeared. But everything got colder, like I was in cold water. I went past the mirror in the hallway, and saw that I looked like a shadow in the dark. And I saw a book, so I picked it up. Then I heard something. Like a child.

Who Are You?

Evie Pattison

What's your least favourite food?
What's your favourite TV show?
The things that make you special,
make you unique?
What's something bad about you?
Like you can't take a critique?
Are you as slow as a snail?
Or as quick as a rabbit?
Or what's that really strange thing
that's a really bad habit?
Are you as strong as an ox?
Or as evil as a fox?
Can you sit in a really tiny box?
What's an interesting fact?
What's the thing that makes your smile grow?
What's the thing that makes your mood really low?
For me, it's a pencil to draw and a pen to write,
a computer and a bed I can sleep in every night.
For me, it's a board game to play, or a friend
to come over and stay.
A little light, something a bit too bright,
for me to see late into the night.

Mint

Evie Shuttleworth

Soft or fierce,
the two defining personalities
of a mint.

To be sweet yet so strong,
to bite back so swiftly.

The second you fall under its charm
it burns your tongue.

So aggressive yet hidden
under a calm, soft layer of sweetness.

He Was Right There

Faiza Ali

Run. Faster, faster! I could feel his eyes on me, trailing me, taunting me, hunting me. I saw him. He saw me. I ran. He ran. Left, right. I ran, he followed. He was faster than me, much faster. I had to get help but who would come? The trees stretched for miles. I could shout but no one would answer. But I had to try. I screamed and screamed. Voice hoarse, I ran but it was no use. He wouldn't stop. Light! Faster. Faster. I ran, wind whipping my hair. But there was no use, he was right there.

Fireworks

Finlay Stoker

I told myself that they were fireworks. Every night, every time another gunshot echoed through my neighbourhood, I told myself they were fireworks. I thought that perhaps if I told myself a lie long enough then one day, I'd truly believe it. That one day it may just be true. It never was. Maybe someday, I'll move somewhere, to a new neighbourhood, where there really are fireworks. Where I don't have to keep up this façade in my head. That's never how it seems to work here, though. People either die here, or they become the ones lighting the fireworks.

Overslept

Finlay Stoker

I could still vividly remember the sound of the alarm, the realisation of what had just happened and the immediate fear that it instilled in me with every step, every wheezing breath, the sound that echoed through my head. I was running faster than I ever had before, as if my life depended on it, because as far as I was concerned it did. The corridors seemed to stretch on for eternity, only interrupted by the various doors which flew past me.

How to Girl

Imaan Ul Haq

Cake and bake your face with makeup to cover up all your
insecurities.

Wear female clothes because wearing clothes that you feel
good in is not 'girly'.

Don't eat too much because we're not supposed to have
weight.

Make sure you always cover up.

Trapped

Imaan Ul Haq

As we enter the car park and the car engine is turned off, I get the feeling of something uncomfortable. I open the car door and leave. She waves goodbye and drives off. Now I'm stuck. I take my time walking down the stairs, dreading what's inside the building. Then I enter. All I can hear are lots of loud footsteps and so many people chatting. The corridors are packed. After escaping the mob, I enter a room. I sit down at a desk and the bell rings. Now I'm trapped for the next six hours of my life. It's time for school.

The Worst Class

Imaan Ul Haq

My class is the worst class in the world. There are so many kids who get sent out of that lesson and lots of kids mess about.

As soon as the late bell goes, the fun begins. The teacher is trying to teach but only a few are listening. Paper airplanes are thrown around the classroom. The teacher is trying to take attendance, but he can't hear over the loud chatter. Two girls in the class are shouting and having their third argument of the day. Some people are on their phones and only a handful of students are getting on with their work. Once the naughty kids have been sent out, they wait outside. While waiting outside they mess with the door, the lights, shout and scream, and run in the corridors. Once everyone has calmed down, the teacher makes us do work in silence. As soon as the bell goes everybody runs out the door. Once everyone has gone, the teacher is secretly regretting teaching our class.

My House

Isaa Ul Haq

I love my house. It is my home, it's my life. I really like my house. The people who live in my house are me, my two older sisters, Haajarah and Imaan, and my mum. My house is my favourite place to be, I just love it. My house is beautiful. My house has all my stuff and some of the best stuff. Some of the things in my house that I love are the sofa, my bed and the TV. I love my house, it's amazing!!

My Life in a Hospital

Isaa Ul Haq

When I was little, I struggled to do a poo. It felt like it was impossible. My mum gave me laxatives to see if they could help but they never worked. One day, my mum took me to the hospital and the doctor told my mum that I was healthy and fine. But up until the age of five I still struggled to do a poo, so my mum took me back to the hospital and this time the doctor told my mum that I needed a stoma bag. This means that my large bowel is sticking outside of my stomach, you then put a removable bag on. This helps me do a poo. So far, I have had ten surgeries and I'm only twelve years old.

Soy

Isabella Curtis

I am a thin shard of glass, fragile and easy to break.
I am trapped in a box, or a cage, unable to get out
or be exposed to the outside world.
I am a piece of paper, easy to write on, but easy to
rip, or hurt others.

But I am a big glass window, strong and easy to see
through.
I am a pen, used to write down my feelings when
nothing else helps, making it easier to express myself.

And when I am at my best, I am a stage – or I am on a
stage – somewhere where I can be somebody else,
in a different world, with a different life, and I can
escape the reality of mine.
I am fashion, sometimes bright, bold and beautiful, other
times more meek and mild.

A Forest and a Bird

Kaydi-Lou Walton

A forest being choked by its own branches, only a lone bird sings a cry for help. A sprawling fortress barricading the bird from warmth, and from sun. From happiness, from freedom. A forest floor where the bird is greeted by a carpet of fine, evergreen needles. The bird always continues to chirp its cry for help, but the beautiful voice is never heard − only echoed through the forest.

A forest, where a gale of wind blew through the trees, filling the bird with the smell of pine and dirt. Drowning in a swarm of nettles, brushing their poison against the fragile bird. The day fell to night and the bird's voice became taciturn.

An infinite field of fireflies hidden by the repulsive woodland. But little did the bird know that behind the suffering there is beauty, fields of flowers deposited by Flora, gardens of gardenia and daisies.

A field of hope,
a field of innocence,
a field of freedom,
a field without fear.

A field unreachable for the lone bird. As the night reaches its peak and the bird's beautiful voice becomes mute, the bird only wants to end the nightmare, but the forest only pushes it further into a world of horror and spite.

The bird was finally free, into a field of poppies. A start of a story, a start of a new fate. One with freedom, one that will never end as the bird writes its own story, attempting to hide from the cruelty of society.

My Little Girl

Kaydi-Lou Walton

A deep tunnel,
a tunnel of mystery and lies,
coated in shallow, murky water.
Police tape hangs from the rusting steel bars,
blocking the entrance.
A reminder of the ticking time.
The time that she has been gone.
No remains were found,
a cold case.
No track of her,
no trace of her.
No detection of my little girl.
I screamed when I got the call.
In the deep tunnel,
they found a clue,
but no sign of life.
She carried Mr Hippo everywhere.
But unlike her,
Mr Hippo was found.
He was no longer grey,
but he was red.
Stained with deep scarlet blood.
A bone piercing through his heart,
a cut slicing through his toe,
a shard of glass in his side.
But there was no trace of who did this,
no trace of who killed my little girl.

A Flash of Memory

Kaydi-Lou Walton

A rush of harsh water as loud as a storm.
The cold water washing over my feet,
The shouts and screams coming from the children playing,
The purple flowers being plucked from the mountains.
I remember his scream,
I remember him falling,
I remember catching him,
I remember harsh rocks cutting my feet,
I remember seeing my dog sprint across the bridge.
A fear shoots through my spine,
The soft grass grazes over the cuts on my feet.
I remember spending time with my family,
I remember their laughs,
I remember their smiles,
I remember the sudden break of peace,
I remember my dog stealing the crisps from my brother,
I remember that day,
I remember my family.

Mannequin

Nadia Khanum

Painting my nails red, his favourite colour. Curling my hair and leaving it free, just what he likes. Putting on my makeup: lipstick, eyeliner, highlighter, glitter, anything I could think of just to impress him. My uniform slips on, my pleated skirt just beneath my bum – would it flatter him? I walk into first period, History. There he is. I glance and flash a smile at him. My heart shatters and bleeds.

Chaos in the Casino (An Excerpt)

Neve Garbutt

As I was backstage, I heard faint noises from the stage. I ran out and saw Chips at the piano. He was playing a song. The kind that plays when you're at a funeral or a wedding. As I sat down next to him, he looked at me. He didn't say anything, just nodded and walked away. He soon returned with three pages of sheet music. He placed them on the stand and walked to get his guitar. He wanted to play the song we wrote when we were four. We weren't good with rhyming back then, so as we got older we changed a few parts, which only made it better. We wrote a lot when we were younger. Now we're so busy with our work in the casino, we hardly know what day it is. We wrote everything and on everything we could get our hands on, but our favourite thing to write was music. We weren't the best at maths or English or science or spellings. But from a young age we both knew how to write music. Chips plays guitar and drums and I play piano and flute. We practised and wrote lots, and so our marks in school weren't that bad. But that changed when we started work at the casino. We both work the night shift, because the casino (to us) is better at night.

Dark Side

Neve Garbutt

Don't hide your dark, evil side,
because doing that is hiding a half of
yourself.

So when stars turn to rocks, dreams turn
to nightmares and love turns to hate,
when light turns to dark, when gain turns
to loss and peace turns to war,
embrace this world, and don't hide this part of yourself.

When you can embrace this part of you,
don't let it take over your mind.
Protect your soul and keep it safe.
So don't hide your dark side,
because it's just as bright as your good side.

Hungry for Knowledge

Poppy Howard

I kept on going, examining the pages from the bewitching and ancient bookshelves which stretched from the floor to the ceiling, unaware I had been walking for hours on end. It was too captivating and I loved the books too dearly to look back. How I regret that now. Now that I am still surrounded by the same old, oak bookshelves lined with the same battered, hardback books, after so much time I feel as if this is the place I will die. How I regret letting the enchanting covers and expertly constructed words hypnotise me. How I wish I had looked back. If only I had looked back.

Feather

Rifha Haque

Feather, that was his name. It really matched him perfectly. He had white, shoulder-length hair made from silk. His lips were soft, so red and plump. His nose was small, like a button. He looked like a doll with his shiny, violet eyes. His glass skin was so pale and smooth... So perfect, right? He always wore white, elegant outfits, he never worried about getting them dirty. He even lived in a wealthy, posh home. Oh dear, was he really perfect? No, he wasn't as kind as a feather, he was rougher than stone.

A Wish Adrift

Rifha Haque

I woke up facing a clear glass wall, in a comfy, violet bed with many cute teddies surrounding me. Wait. A glass wall? I sat up quickly, panicking about where I was. Getting out of my bed, I stumbled up and looked around. I was... in a glass cube? In the middle of nowhere? Was I in the sky? There were clouds but when I looked down there was just water, as if there was land beneath. The cube was floating. No land in sight. Huffing and crying, I remembered where I was, but not why I was here, and I did not know how long it would be until Papa would say I could come back. He texts me on this hologram iPad. Well, he was supposed to...

Murder Mystery

Rifha Haque

An investigation happens after a rumour spread around town. The rumour was that a famous businessman, named Sorren Towlings, had been brutally murdered at 18 Wrightfell Lane. There were four suspects, three of whom were seemingly close to the businessman as he focused more on work rather than communicating because he often thought the latter was a waste of time. Let's read the information on the murder, shall we?

The murder was said to have happened at 9.30 p.m. on Tuesday April 1st 2021. Clearly somebody thought this would make a funny April Fools' joke. Yet no one is laughing. This murder took place at 18 Wrightfell Lane, in the bathroom of Marilyn Finch's house, Mr Towlings' secretary. There, we have our first suspect. She was the one who begged him to join the party at her place, not stopping until he agreed. Sorren also had a friend tag along willingly. Second suspect: Eric Nolan. Eric was one of the people the victim was often spotted with at the party. But he wasn't the one who was seen dragging him upstairs while he was intoxicated. That person was Marilyn's dear sister, Lilith, the third suspect. Lilith was Sorren's childhood friend, the only person he ever interacted with a lot. He must have had one too many shots of alcohol and fell unconscious in the living room, where he left his half-empty bottles of Jack Daniel's and his black, stained tie. Lilith was the person to drag the passed-out businessman upstairs and into the bathroom. She then left, but a tall man was seen to have entered the same bathroom a few minutes later. This last suspect was Lawrence Hydrock, his cousin. Hydrock and Towlings weren't the best of friends, always fought when given the opportunity, claimed Lilith.

Apparently, Lawrence screamed seconds after he entered the bathroom, attracting everyone's attention. Having seen the crime, every guest ran out, crying and panicking. That's when the police arrived and rang Detective Seakhelm, me, to take a look at the scene.

So far, the only evidence we found was: Marilyn's handkerchief, used to silence Mr Towlings' shouts; broken blood-stained glass from the shower, showing instant signs of a struggle; one of Lilith's gloves that she had 'lost'; and a pocket knife that belonged to Eric, which he says he carries with him for 'protection'. But Eric never entered the upstairs bathroom until after the crime had happened. There was also a small paintbrush on the ground. And a message written on the wall: 'If you **SEAK**, I shall **HYDE**'. It's as if the killer knew I was going to be the only detective at the scene. So I felt unsettled. I questioned the suspects about when they last spoke to the victim and why they interacted with him, and these were their responses:

Marilyn: I stopped talking to him as soon as he drank those bottles of alcohol. I knew he never took drinking very well so I didn't wanna be involved... I only wanted him at my party because the man looked so soulless, like he's never had fun in his entire life. You found my handkerchief in his hands?... I never used it, I didn't kill him.

Eric: That pretty girl, what was her name? Lilith? She took him upstairs, haven't heard a word from him since then. I went to the party with him because I wanted to get my mind off... Family... So I thought spending a night at a crazy place would do the trick. Mmm... I brought my knife too but it randomly vanished while I was talking to a stranger.

Lilith: Well, when Sorren had his uncle's business passed down to him, he completely ignored me, then all he's on about

is his stupid work. I took him upstairs because I saw him drunk, cold showers usually sober him up, and I wanted to talk to him afterwards. I must've dropped my glove on the way out.

Lawrence: Never talked to that musty thing in my entire life. He took what was supposed to be mine – you think I'd wanna get *involved* with him? No! I just needed to wee and as soon as I walk in I see his dead body sitting in the shower, blood and glass everywhere. There was a note on the walls too. Looks like someone wrote it with a baby brush.

My Friend

TJ Atkinson

The door slammed shut. I got on my bike and started to pedal. The clashing of my zips on my bag. Once I got to the forest I hid in a nearby den. I heard growling – a wolf had found me. 'Oh no,' I thought. But it just lay on me doing nothing. Then the wolf got up, and so did I, but the wolf started pulling my shirt. Once the bad people had passed and went far away the wolf had stayed all the way through the time. My first friend, my first real friend.

My Yellow Home

TJ Atkinson

The yellow home was a small Beetle car which had burnt down. Me and my friends would sneak off to it when we wanted to hang out and get away from our parents, when we had to socialise with the rest of the family. So this was my yellow home. It smelled of smoke and burnt wood. It was in the woods where we felt at home. We decorated it with fairy-lights and pillows and blankets. We would sneak out of school when we didn't feel like doing the lessons. So my yellow home was the best. Two doors were broken off the body of the car and the fallen leaves would sit around it. The trees would surround the car and we had the perfect view of the sky when the stars were out and shining bright.

We Remember

Group Poem

I remember the first time I held my little sister. I didn't like her
very much.

I remember going on my first holiday in my caravan. I met
someone called Ben who had a pet turtle. I've never seen
him since.

I don't remember when my mum dropped me on my head
outside of McDonald's. Maybe that's why I don't
remember.

I remember eating nettles.

I remember the day I fell ill and was rushed to hospital.

I remember the feeling of fluffiness when I held my cats.

I remember crying because my mum left me to go school for
the first time.

I remember when my grandma said we were going to Whitby
but took us to Disneyland. I was sad that we weren't going
to Whitby.

I remember eating ice-cream with a small wooden spoon – you
could taste the spoon more than the ice-cream.

I remember when I put my sister to sleep.

I remember getting so angry at my brother that I told him he
was adopted.

I remember when my dad cut my hair and got rid of my
fringe. It looked awful but he was so proud.

I remember the time I watched *Of Mice and Men* and I cried
with Mum at 10.30 whilst eating mangoes.

I remember when my cat died and I stroked his stone-cold
corpse.

I remember my friends' laughter when the joke sunk in.

I remember when I had my birthday in Bangladesh.

I remember the joyful screams of children.

I remember when I was little, every Christmas Eve my mum would read me *The Night Before Christmas* before I went to sleep.

I remember the time my Christmas was confiscated.

I remember when I saw my mum cry at the back door after an argument with my dad.

I remember the fox in the garden with its beady little eyes.

I remember being hungry at one in the morning, so I got up and ate an apple.

I remember the hills I would always stare at from my bedroom window.

I remember how small the world seemed, how small every star seemed, before geography came.